NOTHING
BUT
TROUBLE

Betty Ren Wright

drawings by Jacqueline Rogers

Holiday House/New York

Library of Congress Cataloging-in-Publication Data
Wright, Betty Ren.
Nothing but trouble / Betty Ren Wright ; drawings by Jacqueline
Rogers.—1st ed.
p.   cm.
Summary: Vannie tries to make the best of things when she and her
dog Muffy are left with her cranky great aunt on an old farm in Ohio
while Vannie's parents go to California to look for work.
ISBN 0-8234-1175-3
[1. Great-aunts—Fiction.   2. Dogs—Fiction.   3. Country life—
Fiction.]   I. Rogers, Jacqueline, ill.   II. Title.
PZ7.W933No   1995   94-34285   CIP   AC
[Fic]—dc20

FOR
John and Janet,
Erik and Kurt—
and, of course,
for Muffy.

Contents

Chapter 1

A Place to Stay

"This isn't going to work," said Vannie Kirkland's mom for the umpteenth time. "You can't just drop a child at an old lady's door and expect her to say fine-and-dandy. Kids are a lot of trouble."

Vannie's dad whistled "California, Here I Come" through his teeth. He'd been whistling it ever since they left Cleveland.

"If you aren't the world's worst worrier," he said after a while. "Wait and see. Aunt Bert's got to be lonely as all get out, living by herself in the country. She's going to love having Vannie stay with her for a while."

Every time this argument started up again, Vannie scrunched down a little farther in the backseat of the car. Maybe, she thought hopefully, she could make herself shrink away to nothing. Her dad would say, "Well, here's our Vannie, Aunt Bert— come to stay with you while we go off to California." And what do you know; when they looked in the backseat, nobody would be there.

Except Muffy! she reminded herself. Muffy wouldn't disappear. He might be the tiniest white poodle in the whole United States, but he was also the loudest and the fastest. You always knew where he was. At the moment he was perched on a carton full of bedding that took up most of the backseat, snarling and yipping at a semitrailer truck in the next lane.

"For goodness' sake!" Vannie's mom exploded. "Will you please keep that dog

quiet! What's he planning to do, *eat* that semi?"

Vannie didn't answer. Nobody could keep Muffy quiet when he felt like barking. Being small didn't mean a thing to Muffy. That was just one of the reasons Vannie loved him.

She looked out the window and saw that they were in real farm country now. The colors were pretty—green fields, red barns, and silvery silos like towers in a fairy tale.

But where were the people? There was a house every once in a while, with a cluster of farm buildings around it, but she didn't see any people. Just cows—a million cows—and some pigs and, once, a field full of gray sheep with lighter-colored lambs wobbling after their mothers. No wonder Dad's aunt Bert was lonely, if all her neighbors had four legs!

"How much farther is it, for goodness' sake?" Vannie's mom wanted to know. "We've got a long way to go if you expect to make the Mississippi River by dark."

(4)

She sounded tired and unhappy. "We should have called ahead. We should have *warned* your aunt."

Vannie pulled Muffy off the carton and hugged him, even though he squirmed and squealed.

"It's just over the next hill," her dad said, answering the question and ignoring the rest. "Hey there, Vannie, look sharp now. Here's where you're going to spend your summer vacation, lucky girl."

They stopped talking after that. Even Muffy was quiet for a change. The old sedan rattled and rumbled to the top of the hill and started down. Just below them, Vannie saw a little old house set back from the road. Tall trees clustered around it.

Beyond the trees and a shed stood a barn that was at least twice as big as the farmhouse. The roof of the barn had holes in it, but on the side nearest the road there was a huge painting of a gold-colored dog. The dog was leaping over a stream of bright blue water. A row of green hills, all the same size, was lined up behind him, and there were puffy pink clouds overhead.

"What in the world!" Vannie's mom exclaimed. Her dad just shrugged. Now that the moment was here, now that they were actually turning into Aunt Bert's front yard, he looked kind of scared.

"Come on, Vannie," he said, opening the back door of the car. "Get yourself out of there and bring your suitcase."

"No suitcase," her mother said quickly. "Not till we talk. Leave Muffy in the car, too."

She took Vannie's hand as they walked across the grass to the front porch. Behind them, Muffy yelped and battered the car windows, afraid he was being left out of a good time.

Good time! Vannie thought. *Huh!* The closer they got, the more the house looked as if it might fall down any minute.

The porch was a wonder. It stretched across the front of the little house, and it was crammed full of things: a long wooden swing hanging from the roof, a rocking chair, a footstool, a shabby old trunk, a box full of magazines, and a three-legged table that would have tipped over if not for the wooden crate propping it up.

"What in the world!" Vannie's mom said again. "Looks like she must *live* out here."

The door swung open. At first Vannie thought it was someone her own age on the other side of the screen, but when the person spoke, it was in a cracked, used-up kind of voice.

"What is it? Who ya lookin' for?"

Vannie's dad cleared his throat. "It's me, Aunt Bert," he said. "Your nephew Bill. Come to see you on our way to California. How are you? Here's my wife, Grace, and this is our little girl, Vannie."

The screen door flapped open, and a tiny, skinny old lady in blue jeans and a baggy shirt came out on the porch. Her skin was burned potato-brown, and her gray hair was chopped short like a man's. Behind her glasses, her eyes seemed to shoot sparks as she looked at each of the Kirklands in turn.

"Haven't seen any of the family in a month of Sundays," she said after a minute. "If you want to sit awhile, I'll get some lemonade." She motioned toward the swing and the rocker and marched back into the house. Vannie's folks looked at each other and then settled in the swing, making room for Vannie between them.

When Aunt Bert came back, she was carrying a tin tray with glasses on it. The glasses were beautiful, Vannie thought— all red and blue and yellow stripes. Aunt Bert gave them their drinks and then perched on the porch rail facing them.

"Now," she said, "this place is more than fifty miles off the main highway, so I don't believe you just happened by and decided to visit your old aunty. Must have had a reason. Want to tell me what it is?"

Vannie's dad grinned, sort of ashamed. "Well, you're right, Aunt Bert," he said. "And I'm sorry I haven't been here for a long time. The truth is, we've had a streak of bad luck back home, and we've decided it's time to make a fresh start out West. What we're wondering is, can Vannie stay here with you, while we get settled? We'll be sleeping in the car until I get a job and find us a place to live, see. We thought maybe you'd like some company for a while. . . ."

"So that's how the wind blows." Aunt Bert fastened her sparkling eyes on Vannie as if she could see right through her.

"You don't have to say yes," Vannie's mom murmured. "We'll get by."

"I don't *have* to do anything I don't want to do," Aunt Bert retorted. She looked down at her sneakers and then back at Vannie.

"What do *you* say?" she asked. "You think you'd like stayin' here?"

Vannie could feel her father wanting her to say yes. She could feel her mother worrying. If she said, "I sure do want to stay," it would make them both happy. But there was something about Aunt Bert that demanded plain truth.

"Don't know," she said softly. "I never lived in the country. I might get lonesome."

Aunt Bert nodded, as if that was the right answer. She slid down off the porch rail.

"I'll take her," she said. "For a while, anyway. But you'd better send us a little money when you get some. I ain't rich."

"We will!" Vannie's father exclaimed. "We'll surely do that, Aunt Bert. And Vannie's a good girl. You'll see."

"She better be." The old lady didn't smile, but she cocked her head at Vannie. "What's all the ruckus out in your car?"

Vannie jumped up. "It's Muffy," she said, and suddenly she couldn't wait to get her arms around her dog. "I'll get him."

She was halfway across the straggly lawn when Aunt Bert's voice cut the air like a knife.

"Don't bother," she called. "I can see all

I want to see from here. That ain't no dog, that's a powderpuff!"

Vannie stopped and looked back uncertainly.

"What we were thinking is that Muffy could stay here, too," Vannie's dad mumbled. "He's Vannie's good buddy, see, and besides, it's pretty hard traveling with a dog." His anxious smile faded under Aunt Bert's glare.

"I wouldn't have an animal like that if he was solid gold!" she snapped. "If he was solid gold, he wouldn't be yipping his fool head off, but I still wouldn't have him. Nasty little thing. He'd drive my cat crazy! Bet he bites, too."

Vannie felt as if she'd been smacked in the chest. "He does not bite!" she shouted. "He's the best dog in the whole world!" The tears she'd been storing up all the way from Cleveland were about to come pouring out. She gulped and sent Aunt Bert's glare right back at her.

"So you say," Aunt Bert sniffed. She

(11)

turned to Vannie's folks, her hands on her hips. "I told you I'd take the girl, and I will," she said crossly. "But not that dog. I can't abide a silly little beast like that. You make up your mind." And without another word she marched into the house, letting the screen door slam shut behind her.

Vannie's dad took a deep breath. "Well now," he said.

"I knew this wouldn't work," Vannie's mother said. She rubbed her forehead as if it were hurting.

Vannie looked from one of them to the other. "I'm going back to the car," she announced. "That's a mean old lady, and I hate her. I wouldn't stay with her if—if she was solid gold!"

Chapter 2

"That Powderpuff!"

Vannie sat straight as a stick in the driver's seat. With her hands on the steering wheel and her foot on the brake pedal, she felt strong. Too bad her father had the car keys in his pocket! If she had the keys, she could back out onto the highway and head back home. She and Muffy would sleep under the porch of their old house on Glover Street; it was cozy and dark under there. And when Kelly Berman, who lived next door, found out they'd come back, she'd bring them peanut-butter-and-banana sandwiches every day.

Muffy jumped up on the dashboard and barked happily. He thought Vannie could do anything, even drive.

Fifteen minutes had passed since Vannie's folks followed Aunt Bert into the house. What was going on in there? Vannie gripped the steering wheel tighter as the screen door opened. Her mom stepped out. She looked as if she'd like to head back to Cleveland, too.

"Come on in," she called. "And bring Muffy with you."

No! Vannie shouted, but it was the pretend-Vannie who said that, the one who knew how to drive. The real Vannie picked up Muffy and walked slowly to the shabby little house, where her mom was waiting. Together they went inside, and Vannie looked around at the crowded living room. The furniture was old-fashioned and dark. There were lacy covers on the backs of the chairs, and the end tables were covered

(14)

with vases and photographs in cardboard frames. A heater stood in one corner, tall and gleaming, with a bucket of coal beside it.

"Put that beast down on the floor," Aunt Bert ordered. "Let's see what he'll do to my house—as if I can't guess!"

Vannie could guess, too. Muffy was an explorer. The minute his feet touched the floor, he took off like a model airplane, his long ears sticking out like wings. His first leap took him to the arm of the couch, and from there he jumped onto a table. A vase teetered and almost fell as he dived down to a footstool.

"That's enough!" Aunt Bert shrieked. "Stop him this minute!"

Vannie ran toward the footstool, but Muffy had already leaped onto a rocking chair. The chair tipped forward and dumped him on the rug, which surprised him so much that he forgot to keep running.

"You didn't have to yell," Vannie told

Aunt Bert. "Muffy just likes to look around."

"That's right, Aunt Bert." Vannie's dad tried to sound as if he hadn't been worried for even a second. "Muffy's a lively little guy, but he's harmless. And cute as a button, right?"

Aunt Bert made a face. "Cute!" she snorted. "You bring him out in the kitchen now and we'll see. Get ready to grab him again in a hurry," she added grimly. "If he hurts my Elvis, I'll grind him up and have him for breakfast."

She would, too, Vannie thought. They followed Aunt Bert into a sunny kitchen that was about twice as big as the living room. Vannie put Muffy down on linoleum so worn you could hardly see the pattern. They all held their breath.

"Elvis," Aunt Bert snapped. "Wake yourself up and see what we've got out here."

There was a scratchy sound and a whiny meow. Then Elvis appeared from behind the stove. He was a small gray cat, skinny as could be. When he saw Muffy, his eyes lit up and gleamed like Aunt Bert's.

Muffy let out a yelp of pure delight. If there was one thing he liked better than exploring, it was chasing. Before Vannie could stop him, he raced across the kitchen.

"No!" Vannie's mom wailed. "Oh no, oh no! Catch him, Vannie!"

But Vannie was staring at Elvis. Suddenly the gray cat wasn't small anymore. His back was humped, his tail swelled up, and he hissed and spat like a baby dragon. Muffy skidded to a stop with a yelp.

"Well now!" Aunt Bert hooted. "Didn't know old Elvis had it in him. Guess he can take care of himself with that powderpuff!"

"He's not a powderpuff!" Vannie protested as she scooped up her dog.

But Aunt Bert kept laughing. "Whatever he is, he's not goin' to worry Elvis," she chuckled. "Still, that don't mean I'm goin' to like havin' him around. I've known *real*

dogs in my day, and none of 'em looked anything like that!"

Vannie opened her mouth to reply, but no words came out—partly because she was too angry to talk and partly because what Aunt Bert had just said meant that Vannie and Muffy were going to stay.

I won't. You can't make me! the pretend-Vannie yelled. She stamped her foot and glared at Aunt Bert.

The real Vannie hugged her dog as tightly as she could and didn't look at anybody.

Chapter 3

A Night Visitor

Vannie sat on the porch step and stared at the road. Her dad had tooted the horn, and her mother had waved until the car disappeared over the hilltop, but Vannie hadn't waved back. Now she was sorry. Angry but sorry. She knew her folks hadn't *wanted* to leave her behind. Her mother had been crying when they drove away. But they had left her, just the same.

"You want some more lemonade?" Aunt Bert stood just inside the screen door, her hands on her skinny hips. "No use moonin' around out there."

Vannie shook her head.

"Well, you better come on in anyway. You can set the table while I heat up the stew. And bring the beast with you. He wouldn't last two seconds if a raccoon came by."

Vannie gasped and pulled Muffy into her lap. She'd been holding onto his collar, in case he decided to take off after the car, but she'd never thought he might be in danger.

"Would a raccoon really hurt him?" she asked, following Aunt Bert out to the kitchen.

"Tear him to pieces," Aunt Bert said cheerfully. "They have wicked claws. And they don't like to be pestered."

Never, never, never, Vannie promised herself, would she let Muffy go outside without his leash.

There wasn't much meat in Aunt Bert's stew, but the flavor was wonderful. Vannie hadn't realized how hungry she was. She had two helpings, plus a thick slice of bread with strawberry jam on it.

"Bet you don't have bread like that where you come from," Aunt Bert said smugly. "Bet you have that store-bought stuff—soft as marshmallows!"

Vannie shrugged. She *liked* soft, store-bought bread.

"Where'd you get that name of yours, anyway?" Aunt Bert asked a few minutes later. "Vanessa, I s'pose, after some big-shot movie star."

Vannie looked her straight in the eye. "Evangeline," she said proudly. "She's a girl in a poem my mom knows. Evangeline had to leave her home and all her friends and . . ." She gulped, thinking that she and that other Evangeline had a lot in common. "She was a very brave person," she finished unhappily.

Aunt Bert sniffed. "I know all about her," she said. "Have another slice of bread and jam."

A Night Visitor

After supper Vannie helped with the dishes and then wandered around, looking at the house. It didn't take long to see everything. Besides the living room and kitchen, there was a dark hallway leading to the bathroom, Aunt Bert's bedroom, and a tiny spare bedroom stuffed with trunks and boxes.

"Everything in this house is a treasure," Aunt Bert said fiercely. "I keep it just the way my folks had it when they was alive. My mama made those doilies and the quilts and the pillows. Most of the vases and bowls they got when they was married."

Vannie sighed and kept Muffy close to her. With treasures all around and raccoons lurking outside, she wondered how she and her dog were going to stand days and weeks—even months—of living with Aunt Bert.

Then, at bedtime, something good happened. Aunt Bert asked if she'd like to sleep out on the screened-in side porch off the kitchen, instead of in the crowded spare bedroom.

"It's kind of nice out there," she said. "The daybed's lumpy, but you get a good breeze. Sort of like camping. Suit yourself."

Vannie went out on the porch. It was night now, and the barn across the yard was a hulking shadow against the darker sky. About a trillion stars glittered overhead, and the moon looked as if it were trapped in a treetop.

"This is cool," Vannie said. "Really cool."

Aunt Bert looked annoyed. "You won't be cool under my mama's comforter," she snapped. "Too warm, if anything." And she was off to find sheets and the comforter before Vannie could explain what she'd meant by "cool."

After the bed was made up, they watched a game show on the little black-and-white television set in the living room, and then Vannie went to bed. She was so tired, she felt as if she'd *walked* all the way from Cleveland. Besides, she was eager to try out her porch-bed. Aunt Bert produced a burlap bag stuffed with crumpled-up newspapers, which she laid next to the daybed.

"That'll do for the beast," she said, glaring at Muffy. "S'pose he'll bark every time an owl hoots, but he'll have to get used to it."

Vannie dropped one hand over the edge of the bed and held her dog firmly in place till Aunt Bert closed the door. Then she took her hand away. With a bound, Muffy leaped up on the bed. He snuggled down with his head on Vannie's shoulder, just as he had every night at home in Cleveland.

With the door closed, the rest of the house seemed far away. Vannie shut her eyes and listened to the night noises. There were rustlings in the bushes around the house, and a faint honking sound— was that what an owl sounded like?

A far-off train whistled. It was a lonely

sound, making Vannie think of her mom and dad, who must have stopped for the night by now. They would be sleeping in the car, maybe in a park where they could see the moon and the stars. She hoped so. . . .

"What's wrong?"

Vannie jerked awake to find Muffy on his hind legs staring through a screen. He was making little grunting sounds, the way he did when he was scared.

She sat up cautiously, clutching the comforter around her. The yard was bright with moonlight, and tree shadows stretched across the grass. A finger of yellow light streamed around the side of the barn, then disappeared when Muffy began barking.

For a moment Vannie was too frightened to move. She held her breath, but nothing else happened. Desperately, she pulled the dog down on the bed.

"Be *quiet*!" she whispered fiercely. "It's nothing! You'll wake up Aunt Bert."

But she was shaking, and Muffy wasn't fooled. Someone was out there, prowling in the dark. What else could that finger of light have been but the beam of a flashlight?

Chapter 4

Vannie
Finds a Clue

"You can forget all that silliness," Aunt Bert screeched. "I ain't never goin' to do it!"

Vannie sat up so suddenly that Muffy, who had been sound asleep, almost tumbled off the daybed. Sunlight streamed through the windows, and bees sizzled in the bushes. Outside, everything looked green and peaceful, but inside the house Aunt Bert sounded ready to explode.

A deep voice rumbled in the kitchen, too

low for Vannie to make out any words. The minute it stopped, Aunt Bert started screeching again.

"You can just go along home now and stop askin'! I don't know how many times I have to tell you."

The deep voice rumbled once more, and then heavy footsteps clomped through the house and down the front steps. Vannie twisted around in bed and watched a big man in overalls trudge across the front yard to a truck parked in the drive. When Muffy started barking, the man turned around, looking surprised. Then he climbed into the truck and drove away.

"Not a moment too soon!" Aunt Bert appeared at the side-porch door looking flushed and pleased with herself. "If he'd stayed any longer, I might have sicced your beast on him. Then he'd be sorry, ha ha!"

Vannie slid out of bed and followed Aunt Bert to the kitchen. "Who was that?" she asked. "Why don't you like him?"

Aunt Bert gave her a sharp look. "Never said I don't like Jeff Engel," she snapped. "He's all right. He just better not try to tell me how to run my business."

"You sounded mad as a wet hen," Vannie told her. That was one of her mom's favorite expressions.

Aunt Bert snorted. "I don't need anyone tellin' me I should sell him my land, that's all. Jeff's been rentin' land from me for twenty years, and now he wants to buy it. Well, he can just forget that!" She was beginning to sound screechy again. "This place stays the same size it was when my papa farmed it, and that's that. Maybe I can't do the work myself, but I can keep the farm together the way he wanted it."

It sounded odd, hearing an old lady talk about her papa as if she were still his little girl. Vannie thought about that while she dressed in the cluttered little bathroom. When she returned to the kitchen, Muffy was chomping up the last of the stew,

and Aunt Bert was drinking tea and tap-
ping the table with her fingers.

"Eat your breakfast, and then you can
go outside," she said. "Though what you're
going to do all day I can't guess."

"Muffy and I will look for clues," Vannie
told her. "Someone was sneaking around
here last night."

"Rubbish!" Aunt Bert glared at her.
"That's big-city talk. We don't have prowlers."

"You did last night," Vannie insisted.
"Somebody with a flashlight. Muffy saw
the light before I did. Didn't you hear him
barking?"

"That beast would bark at a firefly," Aunt Bert said. "You're imagining
things."

Vannie had never seen a firefly, but she
knew what they were. She was pretty sure
you couldn't mistake one for a flashlight.
As soon as she'd finished her cereal, she
put Muffy on his leash and they went outside. At the corner of the barn, she got

down on her knees and studied the ground.

"If you're looking for footprints, you're wasting your time," scoffed Aunt Bert, just behind her. "Fireflies don't leave any."

"The prowler didn't leave any, either," Vannie said softly. "The ground is too dry."

Aunt Bert put her hands on her hips. "You are one stubborn child," she said. "Come on. I'll show you around the place."

Aunt Bert made a good guide. When she showed Vannie the henhouse, with its half-dozen hens, she described how it used to look long ago, full of chickens and a big rooster who would peck your ankles every chance he got. They stopped at the boarded-up well, and Aunt Bert remembered carrying buckets of water to put out a long-ago grass fire. Out there in the meadow, she'd played with her dog and picked wildflowers for her mama.

As Aunt Bert talked, her voice lost some of its harshness. "Those were the best days," she said. "I couldn't begin to tell you all the good times we had when I was a girl."

The barn was cool and dark inside, its small windows coated with dust. "Used to be cows all in a row down each side," Aunt Bert said. "When I was real little, my papa never wanted me to come in here. He was scared I'd get kicked. But I used to sneak in anyway. Those cows looked big as elephants to me."

"What color were they?"

Aunt Bert looked pleased. "Black and white," she said. "All good milkers, too. Best in the county."

They went out into the sunshine and around to the front of the barn. Vannie looked at the golden dog painted there. Up close, he was bigger than *two* elephants.

"That's Josh," Aunt Bert said. "Josh was the smartest, most beautiful dog that ever lived. My papa paid a travelin' artist to put his picture up there so we'd never forget him. Not that we could," she added. "Josh was a *real* dog." She looked down at Muffy, who was backing away from a grasshopper and yipping nervously. "I smarten the picture up once in a while," she went on, shaking her head. "The colors get kind of washed out otherwise."

On the way back to the house, Vannie saw a little scrap of silver paper close to the corner of the barn.

"Look!" She held it up proudly. "This is a clue. Somebody dropped a chewing-gum wrapper last night. Unless it's yours," she added cautiously.

"Of course it's not mine!" Aunt Bert said. "I never chewed gum in my life. Your pa probably dropped it yesterday."

Vannie sniffed the paper. "My dad and I chew spearmint," she said. "This is cherry."

Aunt Bert wasn't interested. "I've got work to do," she grumbled. "Can't be wanderin' around out here all morning." Now that she'd stopped talking about the old days, her voice was tired and cracked again.

Vannie Finds a Clue

When Aunt Bert was back in the house, Vannie sat down on the grass and pulled Muffy into her lap. She looked at the gum wrapper. It was a clue. She knew it was. But she didn't know what to do about it.

Chapter 5

Slashed!

The next day Aunt Bert announced that they were going to town for groceries.

"Doughnuts?" Vannie suggested helpfully. "Soda pop? Pretzels? Peanut butter?"

Aunt Bert didn't look up from the list she was making. "Whole-wheat flour, rice, and beans," she read aloud. "Peanut butter's okay, I guess. I don't have cash for frills, you know. Besides, that other stuff will rot your teeth."

She added a few more items and then popped the list into her thin, black handbag.

"Leave the beast at home," she ordered. "I can't drive with him racketing around. Elvis is outside, so we can close the door to the kitchen."

Vannie filled Muffy's bowl with fresh water and gave him lots of extra hugs so he wouldn't feel bad about being left behind. But when she went outside, she saw that Aunt Bert's car was stopped halfway out of the shed, where she kept it. The old lady was glaring at a back tire.

"Flat!" she said. "Must have run over a nail last time I was out."

"Who's going to fix it?" Vannie wondered.

"Who do you think?" Aunt Bert took off her sweater and tossed her handbag through the open window of the car. "You go about your business," she said briskly. "But don't go far. It won't take long to put on the spare."

Vannie could hardly believe it. Aunt Bert set to work as if she'd been fixing cars all her life.

"My papa taught me," she said when she noticed Vannie watching. "Now you just go along somewhere. It makes me nervous havin' someone peerin' over my shoulder."

Vannie went into the house to get Muffy. He was so glad to have her back, he leaped all over her. She fastened the leash to his collar, and they went out the front door and across the yard to the road.

The day was bright, the air feather soft. Muffy tugged in one direction, then another, trying to sniff everything that caught his eye. Together they climbed the steep hill that Vannie's mom and dad had taken when they drove away.

As they reached the top, a fat toad flopped out of the tall grass onto the gravel. Muffy yelped and scooted toward it just as a bicycle hurtled over the hill. The rider saw Muffy's leash stretched in front of

her and tried to brake, but it was too late. Bicycle, Vannie, and Muffy all went down in a dusty, noisy heap.

Vannie scrambled to her feet first. "Are you okay?" she asked the bike rider anxiously. "I'm really sorry."

"I'm all right." The girl was about Vannie's age, with hair as long and kinky-curly as Vannie's was short and straight. "Except my knee," she added. Then she grinned at Muffy, who had recovered from his surprise and was sniffing the scraped knee.

"That's a neat dog!" she exclaimed. "You know what, I had a stuffed toy dog that looked just like him when I was little. What's his name?"

Vannie told her. "Is your bike broken?"

"No way." The girl picked up the bike and straightened the wheels. "I've fallen off this thing about a million times, and it's still okay. My mom says my bike and I belong together because we both get a new bump every day."

Vannie helped the girl brush herself off. Then they walked down the hill together. She found out that the girl's name was April Johnson, and the bike's name was Wrecko. April lived on a farm about a quarter-mile down the road.

"We have a creek behind our house, and I have a tree house. My big brother built it, but now it's mine!"

Vannie explained that she and Muffy were visiting Aunt Bert Kirkland for a while—she didn't know how long.

April stopped short when she heard that. She looked down the driveway to where Aunt Bert was examining the tire that leaned against the car.

"You live with *her*?" she whispered. "Does she yell at you a lot?"

Vannie shrugged. "Some." She felt uncomfortable talking about Aunt Bert.

"Maybe she'll let you come over to my house tomorrow," April said, squinting down the driveway. "Ask her. And bring Muffy."

(43)

Vannie promised she would call April as soon as they got back from town. It was exciting to find a friend so unexpectedly—especially one who liked Muffy a lot.

As it turned out, they didn't go to town after all. When Vannie returned to the car, Aunt Bert was hoisting the damaged tire into the trunk.

"There's a long tear in it," Vannie said, running a finger over the jagged place. "Did you find the nail?"

"A nail didn't make a cut like that," Aunt Bert said. "Use your head, girl." She looked tired, and there were beads of sweat on her forehead. "If this was the big city, I'd say that tire's been slashed, but such stuff doesn't happen here. Not ever! I probably drove over a sharp piece of metal last time I went to town."

Slashed! Vannie thought about the beam of light she and Muffy had seen around the side of the barn. She reached into her jeans pocket and felt the gum wrapper folded up tight.

"Anyway, what's done is done," Aunt Bert continued. "I'm way too beat to drive into town now, that's for sure. Those lugs were rusted just awful."

"I met a girl called April Johnson up on the hill," Vannie said. "She asked Muffy and me to come over tomorrow. Is that okay?"

"Suit yourself," Aunt Bert replied. She wiped her face with the corner of her shirt and looked down at the tire one more time. Then she slammed the trunk and went back to the house.

Chapter 6

Witches
on the Windows

Every day Vannie learned something new.

She learned that Aunt Bert liked things *neat*.

She found out that if you made a mistake, it didn't matter much how many times you said, "I'm sorry." When Muffy knocked over a vase and broke it, Aunt Bert wouldn't let him back in the living room for a week. "That beast is worse than an earthquake!" she screeched. Vannie pointed out that the vase had been cracked to begin with, but that just made her aunt angrier.

One day when they went into town for groceries, Vannie asked if they could stop at the Hamburger Hut for lunch. That was when she learned how Aunt Bert felt about fast-food restaurants.

"That stuff'll kill you!" she exclaimed as they drove home to a lunch of bean soup and homemade bread. Vannie liked Aunt Bert's soup, but she'd just about *die* for a cheeseburger.

In the afternoons, playing with the newest litter of kittens in the Johnsons' barn, Vannie got lots of sympathy from April.

"How can you stand living there?" she exclaimed. "That old lady's so crabby!"

"Not always," Vannie said honestly. But at night, curled up in her porch bed, the bad times were easier to remember than the good ones. Vannie wondered how much longer it would be before her folks came back for her. She began to feel as if she'd been living with Aunt Bert forever.

(47)

One morning a howl of rage woke her. *Now what!* Had Muffy broken something else when no one was looking? She jumped out of bed and dashed into the kitchen. Aunt Bert was standing at a window, her face as red as a ripe tomato.

"LOOK AT THAT!" she roared. "When I catch the scallawag who did that, he'll be sorry!"

Each of the three kitchen windows had a picture drawn on it. One was a drawing of a stick-figure witch in a pointed hat. She was riding a broomstick, and there was a cat behind her. In the second, the witch towered over a smaller stick-person whose hair stuck out in every direction. There was a little animal between them that could have been a rat. Vannie guessed it was supposed to be Muffy.

In the third picture the witch was lying down with her toes pointed straight up. She looked dead.

"This ain't one bit funny!" Aunt Bert fumed. She narrowed her eyes at Vannie, as if drawing on windows was a city-girl trick. Then she stormed to the broom closet for the bucket and the bottle of vinegar she used for cleaning.

"I won't eat a bite till that shameful mess is gone," she announced.

The cleaning-up took a long time, because the pictures were drawn with something very sticky. Vannie wanted to help, but Aunt Bert wouldn't let her. By the time all three windows were sparkling again, the old lady was white-faced and trembling.

"You'll have to fix yourself some lunch," she told Vannie. "I'm going to lie down." And off she went to her bedroom, muttering under her breath.

After she'd left, the kitchen was very quiet. Vannie was scared, for a couple of reasons. She was scared because now she knew for sure that she hadn't imagined the prowler. It was someone who could come so quietly that even Muffy didn't wake up. And she was scared because

Aunt Bert looked as if all that anger and hard work had made her really sick. Perhaps the prowler had cast a spell on her and she was going to die. The thought sent chills up and down Vannie's spine.

She went to the refrigerator and looked inside. Maybe Aunt Bert wouldn't be so pale and shaky if she ate something. A bowl of leftover mashed potatoes and a couple of wieners reminded Vannie of one of her favorite meals back in Cleveland. She found a can of tomato soup in the cupboard—it was the only kind of store soup Aunt Bert would buy—and heated it with the wieners sliced into it. Then she poured the mixture over a scoop of warmed-up mashed potatoes.

A few minutes later, she tiptoed down the hall, carrying the old tin tray. Aunt Bert was asleep, but her eyes flew open when Vannie set the tray on the bedside table.

"What's all this?" she demanded. "What have you been up to?"

"I made lunch," Vannie explained. "You

said it was all right. And you'd better eat it because you didn't have any breakfast."

Aunt Bert stared at the plate. "Looks all right," she admitted finally. "But I'll have it in the kitchen, thank you. I don't hold with eating in bed."

As she ate her own plateful of potatoes and soup, Vannie felt a little less scared. The lunch tasted like home. And Aunt Bert was looking more like herself every minute.

"Well, that's one way to get rid of leftover mashed potatoes," the old lady said when her plate was empty. "Now, the next thing we have to do is find out who messed up those windows." She said "we" as if she and Vannie were partners.

Just then, Muffy came into the kitchen from the living room with a scrap of cloth dangling from his mouth.

"What's that?" Aunt Bert demanded. "What's that he's got?" She pushed back her chair and rushed into the living room. When she returned, she was waving a sofa pillow over her head.

(51)

"Ruined!" she screeched. "My mama's favorite pillow that she worked on one whole winter. That beast has chewed the lace right off it. Oh, just wait'll I get my hands on him!"

She made a grab for Muffy, who scuttled behind the stove and out again, yipping furiously. (He'd forgotten about Elvis.)

"Muffy didn't mean it!" Vannie wailed. "He's sorry!"

But of course it was no use. Aunt Bert turned and stomped out of the kitchen and back to her bedroom, the ruined pillow clutched to her chest.

Vannie sank into a chair. When Muffy leaped into her lap, she fed him a slice of wiener dripping with tomato soup, even though she knew he deserved a scolding, not a treat. What was the use of scolding? What was the use of *anything*?

If she had known where her mom and dad were, she'd have started hitchhiking to California that very afternoon.

Chapter 7

Muffy, Where Are You?

The next morning Muffy was gone.

Vannie wasn't worried when she woke to find the dog missing from his usual curling-up spot on the daybed. He had gotten up early before. But when she slid out of bed and padded out to the kitchen, Muffy wasn't there, either. Aunt Bert sat at the table drinking tea, with a grumpier-than-usual expression on her face.

"He ain't in there," she said when Vannie peeked nervously into the living room.

"You might as well know, the beast skedaddled. I was sweepin' dust out the back door, and he just flew out between my legs."

Vannie stared at her. Then she raced across the kitchen and out the door.

"No use lookin' out there, either," Aunt Bert shouted after her. "I've been all around the place. I told you he skedaddled."

Vannie ignored her. "Muffy!" she cried. "Muffy, come here!" Panic made her voice choked-up and weird. Her bare feet flew over the dew-wet grass. Around the barn she dashed, then inside and down the long aisle where the black-and-white cows had once stood. . . . Outside again and into the garage shed—but why would Muffy go in there? Maybe he was out in the meadow, where the tall grass could hide a hundred little white dogs.

"Muffy! Muffy!"

"Come on back and eat your breakfast." Aunt Bert suddenly appeared beside her.

"You can't run all over creation in your pajamas. After you eat, I'll help you look for the beast."

Vannie burst into tears. She couldn't help it. "I don't want breakfast!" she sobbed. "Who cares about breakfast!"

Aunt Bert shook her head. "Just the same," she said and took Vannie by the shoulder, turning her around. "Maybe he'll come back by himself while you're eatin'."

Still sniffling, Vannie let herself be led back into the house. She stood at the screened window looking out while she took off her pajamas and got dressed. When Aunt Bert set a bowl of oatmeal in front of Vannie, she picked it up and went outside to the porch steps, where she could eat and watch the yard at the same time.

"Don't you want some cinnamon and milk on that?" Aunt Bert asked from the kitchen. Vannie shook her head. There was a terrible emptiness inside of her that oatmeal couldn't fill.

When she'd eaten, she and Aunt Bert

walked around the barn together, past the painting of Josh the Perfect Dog, and all around the shed. In the distance, a tractor crawled across a patch of brown earth where nothing was growing.

"Is that Mr. Engel?" Vannie asked.

"Yep." Aunt Bert looked sternly at the tractor. "What about it?"

"Could you call him later and ask if he saw Muffy this morning? Running across the fields, maybe?"

Aunt Bert made a face. "I could, I s'pose," she said. "But the less I talk to that man these days, the better I like it. If I call him, he'll maybe think I've changed my mind about sellin'. But I'll ask," she added, after a sidelong glance at Vannie. "Later. We've done all we can do now, for sure. Might as well go back in the house and start the cleanin'."

Vannie looked at Aunt Bert to see if she was serious. She was. She was going to scrub floors and dust and polish just as if this was an ordinary day!

Because it is an ordinary day for her, she thought. *She hates Muffy. She's probably glad he's gone!*

"I'm going over to April's house," Vannie announced. "She'll help me look."

Aunt Bert shrugged. "Go ahead. But the beast could be a long way from here by now. If he was near, I expect he'd be home by now, getting into mischief."

Vannie tightened her lips. A picture jumped into her mind: Aunt Bert sweeping the dust out the kitchen door, sweeping, sweeping—sweeping Muffy outside, too. It was such a terrible idea that Vannie couldn't bear it. With a sob, she raced across the yard toward the highway, as fast as she could go.

Chapter 8

Who's There?

April was a good searcher. She led Vannie to a cave at the base of the hill between Aunt Bert's farm and the Johnsons' land, then to a dry well partly covered with pieces of board. After that, they looked under April's front porch, where there was a hole just big enough for a small dog to crawl through. Each time April thought of a new place to search, Vannie felt a surge of hope. With each disappointment, she felt worse.

"He's gone," she said at last, trying not to cry. "He's really gone."

April squeezed her hand. "Maybe your aunt could put an ad in the town paper next week," she said comfortingly.

Next week! Vannie bit her lip. She wanted her dog back now!

By the end of the afternoon, they were hot and tired.

"We could look along the creek," April suggested. "And go wading at the same time."

Vannie was too unhappy to care what they did next. Still, when they reached the creek, she had to admit that the clear water looked inviting. The girls kicked off their sneakers and waded in.

"Too bad we didn't wear our bathing suits under our shorts," April said.

Vannie started to say she didn't have a bathing suit, but at that moment April stumbled. Vannie reached out to grab her, and before they knew it they were both sitting on the rocky bottom, cool water tickling their chins.

"Ooh, that feels good!" April gasped.

Vannie didn't feel like laughing, but a giggle bubbled up inside her anyway. She bent forward and dipped her face into the water with her eyes open. It was like looking into another world.

"Oh, man, what a pair of drowned rats!"

Vannie sat up quickly and struggled to her feet. April was already standing, hands on hips, glaring at the two boys on the bank.

"You get away from here, Matt," she shouted. "This is private property."

"So?" The bigger boy shrugged and looked around. "Where's your dumb dog?" he asked Vannie. "Is he scared of water?"

"How do you know about my dog?" Vannie demanded.

The boy snickered. "My dad told me, that's how. He said he's one of those pesky little yippers. So, where is he?"

"He's lost!" Vannie snapped. "And he's

not a pesky yipper. He's a very smart dog."

"It's none of your business anyway," April chimed in. "You'd better get out of here right now. We're busy looking for Muffy, and we don't have time to talk to you."

Both boys laughed. "Funny way to look for a dog," said the one called Matt. "Sitting in the creek! You know what I think?" He made a terrible face at Vannie. "I think that mean old witch you live with probably got rid of him. I bet she *ate* him!"

Vannie stared at him.

"I said get out!" April shouted. "Get out right now!" She reached down with both hands and swept a wave of water up on the shore.

The boys jumped back, laughing, and then shuffled away, poking each other as they walked. April shouted after them till they disappeared beyond the willows that lined the creek.

"Who are they?" Vannie asked when her friend stopped to catch her breath.

"Matt Engel's the tall one," April said. "His dad farms your aunt's land. Billy Barker tags after Matt all the time." She cocked her head at Vannie. "Hey, what's the matter? You don't believe what he said about your aunt, do you? She wouldn't . . . she wouldn't eat—"

"Of course she wouldn't," Vannie snapped. "But he called her a witch—why did he say that?"

"He was just teasing," April assured her. "Matt always says dumb stuff. I might call your aunt a witch myself, but I wouldn't mean it."

Vannie didn't argue. Muffy was still lost, and that was all she cared about. Suddenly, the water swirling around her knees made her shiver.

"I'd better go," she said. "Thanks for helping me look."

"We can do it again tomorrow," April offered. "I'll think of some more places."

"Okay." Vannie tried to sound hopeful, but it was no use. They weren't going to

find Muffy. He must have been dog-
napped, or maybe he'd met a raccoon and
he was dead! If he could have, he would
have come back by now. She was sure of
it.

As soon as supper was over, Vannie said
she was going to bed. She felt numb—so
numb that she hardly noticed the plate of
fresh brownies in the center of the table.
She wasn't hungry, and she didn't feel like
watching television.

"Go ahead then," Aunt Bert said. She
helped herself to a second brownie, as if
to show that *she* knew a good thing when
she saw it, even if Vannie didn't. "You'll
feel better after a night's sleep."

Vannie doubted it. Sleeping on the
porch had been fun when she could put
out her hand and feel Muffy beside her.
Now, lying on the daybed and staring out
at a zillion stars, she felt miserably small
and lonely.

When sleep finally came, bad dreams
came with it. First, she was standing alone

in the dark when a prowler as big as a giant appeared at the corner of the barn. Vannie woke up, her heart pounding, and then slipped back into dreams again. She was at the side of the road as a car rattled by, with Muffy barking and leaping against the back window. Once again she woke, close to tears. The dream had felt so real.

The scuffling sound began so softly that at first Vannie didn't notice it. When she did, she realized it was coming from the front of the house. Someone—or something—was moving around on the front porch.

She felt a flicker of hope. Maybe—just maybe—Muffy had come home. Maybe he was scratching at the front door this very minute. . . .

She slipped out of bed and tiptoed across the side porch to the kitchen. Should she wake Aunt Bert? She was trying to decide when she heard a thud in the front of the house. Then Aunt Bert appeared in the hallway like a little white ghost. She was

(67)

carrying a flashlight with the beam pointed at the floor.

Together they tiptoed across the living room toward the front windows.

"Who's there?" Aunt Bert's shriek was as startling as a siren in the stillness. She swung the flashlight upward and pointed the light at a window.

The face on the other side of the glass didn't look human. It had no nose, no mouth, no ears—just two eyes that glared in at them for a second and then vanished.

Chapter 9

No Room for a Dog

"He was wearin' a ski mask," Aunt Bert said shakily. "The nerve of him, lookin' right in at us like that! I've a good mind to—" She started toward the front door, but Vannie grabbed the sleeve of her nightgown.

"Don't go out there," she pleaded. "He might—he might hurt you!"

Aunt Bert pulled away. "That dirty coward ain't goin' to hurt me!" she stormed. But she sank into the rocking chair as she said it and started to rock furiously.

Vannie tiptoed back to the window and peeked out. "I think he's gone," she said after a minute. "It's quiet out there." She could have added that the crowded front porch looked somehow different, but she didn't want to get Aunt Bert started again. "We'd better call the police."

"The sheriff, not the police," Aunt Bert corrected her. "And no, we aren't goin' to call him. I don't need some deputy thinkin' I can't take care of my own." The rocker slowed just a little. "You go back to bed. Sleep in my room if you don't want to be out on the porch. I'm stayin' right here to watch till the sun comes up."

Vannie got a pillow and blanket from her bed and returned to the living room.

"I'm going to watch with you," she said. She moved the fancy pillows from the couch to a chair and lay down.

"Do what you want," Aunt Bert said. All

of a sudden the fire seemed to have gone out of her. She sounded exhausted.

After that the house was so quiet Vannie could hear the clock ticking in the kitchen. She stared at the windows till her eyes ached, but the terrifying masked face didn't come back. *We're like pioneers,* she thought, remembering a story she'd read in school last year. *This is our little log cabin, and there're wolves and bears all around it.* She shivered and pulled the blanket up to her chin.

When she opened her eyes again, gray morning light filled the window. Aunt Bert was unlocking the front door. Vannie kicked off her blanket, and together they went out on the porch.

"Oh! My!" Aunt Bert gasped. "Oh, the wickedness of it!" She hurried down the steps to where the old rocking chair lay on its side. "My papa's chair, ruined! Oh, wait till I get my hands on that villain!"

Vannie looked around in dismay. The three-legged table was upside down on the porch. The vase of wildflowers that had stood on the table was broken in a hundred pieces. All over the yard, magazines flapped in the breeze or just lay limp, dew-soaked. The swing that hung from the porch roof was partly unhooked and tilting.

"Big-city wickedness out here in the country," Aunt Bert grumbled. "I never thought it could happen!"

Vannie groaned. "If Muffy had been here, he would have barked and scared the prowler away."

Aunt Bert just sniffed.

Together they carried the broken rocking chair back up on the porch and turned the table right-side up. After that, Vannie wandered around the yard gathering magazines and catalogs, while Aunt Bert swept up the broken glass. They worked silently, not looking at each other.

"You'd best move into the spare bedroom for a while," Aunt Bert said when they were back in the house. "I don't want you out on the side porch with such things goin' on."

As soon as they'd had breakfast, Vannie set off again for the Johnson farm, eager to escape the quiet of the little house. She didn't tell April what had happened—Aunt Bert would hate being talked about—but all day long, as they searched for Muffy, her thoughts kept going back to the prowler in the ski mask. What if he returned and did something awful? Surely Aunt Bert would have to call the sheriff then, whether or not she wanted to.

When Vannie got home, Aunt Bert had hooked up the porch swing and was sitting in the middle of it. She had a poker across her knees.

"Didn't find him, huh?" she commented as Vannie came slowly up the steps. "Well, you might as well quit lookin'. I told you if the beast was anywhere around here, he'd have shown up by now."

Vannie knew she was right, but she didn't want to hear the words. She especially didn't want to hear them from Aunt Bert.

"A letter came," Aunt Bert said suddenly. "From your ma. It's in on the kitchen table. I didn't open it 'cause it's addressed to both of us."

Vannie raced inside and back again. When she tore open the envelope, a twenty-dollar bill fluttered out.

"You read it out loud," Aunt Bert said. "I don't have my glasses."

The letter was very short.

Dear Vannie and Aunt Bert,

I'm sorry I haven't written, but there wasn't any news till now. Two days ago Dad got a job delivering pizzas, and next week I'll start waiting on tables part-time. The money won't be much, but it'll do. We're in a dinky little apartment. You'll have to sleep in the living room when you get here, Vannie, but maybe we can find something nicer later on. I hope things are okay with you both. Be a good girl, Vannie—I know you will be. Your dad will be back to get you at the end of the summer, before school starts. I love you.

Mom

Vannie looked over the letter carefully, to make sure she hadn't missed anything. The handwriting made her mom seem real again.

"She needn't have sent the money," Aunt Bert said after a minute. "We'd have managed. But it'll come in handy."

Vannie nodded. She felt a little bit more cheerful. Her folks had jobs. Her father was coming to get her. Now, if she could just find Muffy. . .

"You notice she doesn't speak of the dog," Aunt Bert said, almost as if she'd been reading Vannie's mind. "Maybe it's just as well the beast took off. There's goin' to be no room for a noise-box dog in that apartment."

Vannie gasped. She couldn't have felt worse if Aunt Bert had hit her.

"There will too be room!" she exploded. "You're mean!"

Aunt Bert looked at her in surprise. "No need to get in a snit," she said, tucking the twenty-dollar bill in her shirt pocket. "You can get some other kind of pet, I s'pose. A goldfish, maybe."

Chapter 10

All Alone

A goldfish! Vannie was mad enough to spit. As if a goldfish could take Muffy's place! She ran outside, still clutching the letter, and across the yard to the barn. There, in the cool, dim light, she read the letter again.

It was true that her mom hadn't mentioned Muffy, but that didn't mean anything. Her folks wouldn't expect her to give up Muffy. They wouldn't.

But what if I don't find him?

All Alone

Over the next few days, Vannie spent as much time with April as possible. She helped with chores at the Johnson farm, and the girls took turns riding Wrecko. Once Mrs. Johnson took them into town, and they stopped at the Hamburger Hut for lunch. But always, no matter what else she was doing, Vannie never stopped watching for Muffy.

"Did you ask your aunt to put an ad in the paper?" April wondered.

Vannie shook her head. How could she ask for help from a person who said it was a good thing Muffy was gone?

"I don't think I should bother her," she said carefully. "She doesn't feel so good."

It was true that Aunt Bert was pale and even more short-tempered than usual, probably because she sat up for hours waiting for the prowler to come back. Night after night, Vannie fell asleep to the creak-creak of the living-room rocker. Once she was awakened by a strange snuffling. When she tiptoed into the living room,

Aunt Bert was there in the chair, sound asleep and snoring. The electric lantern was at her feet, and the poker lay across her knees.

She looked small and helpless, sitting in the big chair with her felt slippers barely touching the floor. But she wasn't helpless, Vannie reminded herself. And she wasn't sorry Muffy was gone, either.

"This afternoon's my monthly ladies' meeting," Aunt Bert announced at breakfast one morning. "You better stay at the Johnsons' till five o'clock. I'll be sure to be home by then. I don't want you here alone until we get this business settled." "This business" was what she called the prowler.

Vannie arrived at the Johnson farm after lunch and discovered a surprise in the barn. April's father had brought home a pony from the county auction. The pony was white with patches of chocolate brown. He had a muzzle as soft as silk.

Vannie and April took turns riding him, around the barnyard at first and then all the way to the creek and back. It was so much fun that Vannie stopped thinking about Muffy for minutes at a time.

Five o'clock came too fast. When April's mom rang the dinner bell outside the back door, Vannie set off at a run down the highway. She didn't want to be late. Aunt Bert was like a firecracker these days, always ready to blow up.

The house had an odd, unlived-in look when Vannie turned in to the yard. Her steps slowed as she tried to figure out what was wrong. Then she knew. All the windows and the front door were closed up tight. She went around to the back and found that door locked, too.

Vannie had a house key on a ribbon around her neck. Aunt Bert had given it to her, but she felt funny using it, almost as if she were the prowler, letting herself in where she wasn't welcome.

"Aunt Bert? I'm home."

All Alone

The house was hot and stuffy. Vannie could smell the chicken soup they'd had for lunch. She peeked into the living room and then tiptoed down the hall to the bedroom. Aunt Bert wasn't there.

The telephone rang, and Vannie nearly jumped out of her sneakers. She hurried to the kitchen and picked up the phone before it could ring again.

"All right, you listen to me now." Vannie felt a wave of relief, even though Aunt Bert sounded crankier than usual. "I won't be home for a while, 'cause I've had another flat tire. Don't know if it was cut last night," she added before Vannie could ask. "I'm at Mrs. Calley's place, and her boy's gone to find me a new tire and get the old one patched. So I'll be a while." She paused. "Are you listenin'?"

"Yes."

"Then go right this minute and lock the door. Keep the windows closed, too. I don't like you bein' there alone, but there's nothin' I can do till the boy gets back. You eat somethin' if you're hungry, and I'll be home soon as I can get there."

"I'll be okay."

" 'Course you will, if you do as I say." Vannie realized that Aunt Bert wasn't just cranky; she was scared. She must be worrying about the prowler all the time, just the way Vannie worried constantly about Muffy.

It was a weird feeling being alone in the house. If Muffy had been there, Vannie wouldn't have minded one bit, especially since the sun was still shining. But Muffy *wasn't* there, and the house smelled of more than chicken soup. It smelled empty.

She hoped Mrs. Calley's boy would bring back the new tire in a hurry. Feeling like a pioneer, with wolves and bears sneaking around your cabin, was *really* scary when you were all alone.

Chapter 11

Vannie
Takes Charge

Nibbling on a peanut-butter-and-pickle sandwich, Vannie watched the long summer evening fade into darkness. After a while she turned on the television, but her eyes kept moving from the screen to the living-room windows. What would she do if she saw someone looking in at her? And why was it taking so long to buy a new tire?

At nine o'clock the phone rang again.

"You're all right then." Aunt Bert's flat, used-up voice sounded far away.

"I'm okay," Vannie said. "Nothing's happened."

"Well, I didn't expect it would," Aunt Bert snapped. "But you can't be too careful. Mrs. Calley's boy had a hard time finding the right-size tire, and when he finally got back and put it on, the battery was dead as a doornail."

"Oh." Vannie wondered if she was going to be alone all night.

"It's all tended to now," Aunt Bert continued. "I'll be home in no time, less'n the whole engine falls out. Got somethin' to tell you, but it can wait." The receiver clicked.

Vannie went back to the television. The house didn't seem quite so empty now that she knew she wouldn't be alone much longer. At nine-thirty she switched off the TV and stood at the front window. Any minute now, the headlights of Aunt Bert's old car would swoop over the hill and tunnel down through the darkness. *Before I count to twenty,* Vannie promised herself.

She started counting slowly: *One, two, three, four* . . .

Out of the corner of one eye, she saw a wink of light in the space between the back of the shed and the barn. A moment later she saw it again, a thin pencil of light, hastily covered.

The prowler was back.

Vannie's heart thumped like a drum. She wondered if she should call the sheriff. Aunt Bert wouldn't, but Aunt Bert wasn't here. . . .

She ran to the kitchen and looked out a side window. Something was moving toward the barn. It looked like a monster! She blinked and looked again. The monster turned into two people carrying something long and narrow between them.

Hardly breathing, Vannie tiptoed to the kitchen door and eased it open. There were whispers, then a laugh. More whispers. "That mean old witch—" She'd heard those words, and that laugh, before.

Scared, but angry, too, she opened the

(87)

door a little farther and slipped out into the night. Aunt Bert had told her to stay inside, but she *had* to find out for sure if one of the prowlers was Matt Engel. Just a quick look, she told herself. Then she'd run back to the house and lock the door.

She tiptoed to the corner of the shed and peered across the yard to the barn. At first she couldn't be sure of what was happening, but gradually her eyes became used to the dark. A ladder was propped against the side of the barn. One of the dark figures was climbing to the top, holding a flashlight. The other was holding the ladder steady. They were doing something to the painting of Josh the Perfect Dog!

Vannie was shocked to her toes. Of all Aunt Bert's treasures, she knew the barn painting was the most precious. In an instant, she forgot her plan to take one quick look at the intruders and then run back to safety. Soundlessly, she raced across the yard and threw herself on the shoulders of the person holding the ladder.

"Hey!"

The prowler staggered backward, pulling the ladder with him. Vannie dropped to the ground and scuttled aside as the ladder swung outward, tossing the second prowler on top of the first. The flashlight hurtled across the grass. Vannie snatched it up and turned it on the struggling figures. Their faces were covered by ski masks, but there was no mistaking Matt Engel's roar of surprise and pain.

"Get off me, stupid!"

"Get off, yourself!"

At that moment white light swept across the yard as a car turned in from the highway.

"Here comes the sheriff!" Vannie shrieked. She threw the flashlight at the figures on the ground and raced across the yard and around the shed to meet Aunt Bert.

Chapter 12

Donkey Ears

"Sheriff? What sheriff? What are you yellin' about?" Aunt Bert scrambled out of the car. "Didn't I tell you to stay inside?"

"The sheriff! It's the sheriff!" Vannie shouted again. "Come on, Aunt Bert," she added in a whisper. "The prowlers came back—two of them!—and I know who one of them is!"

They hurried along the side of the shed and peeked around the corner. The barnyard was empty. Vannie scooped up the flashlight from the grass and pointed it at the barn.

"That ladder!" Aunt Bert exclaimed. "What's a ladder doin' here? And what's that?" She pointed to a big blob of something in the grass with an overturned can next to it.

"It's paint," Vannie said. "There were two boys, and one of them was Matt Engel, Aunt Bert. They were doing something to the picture of Josh."

Aunt Bert gasped, as if the words had knocked the breath right out of her.

"Go on in the house and get the big electric lantern," she ordered after a minute. "Hurry up now!"

Vannie raced across the grass and into the house. When she returned, Aunt Bert was standing where she'd left her.

"Shine it up there on the wall," she ordered. "Slowly now! Start at one side and go all the way across."

Vannie held her breath as the lantern beam moved over bright green hills and blue skies. There was Josh's feathery tail, his golden coat, the proud head. . . .

The light wavered and stopped.

"Oh, those villains!" Aunt Bert shrieked. "Those wicked scamps!"

Vannie stared at the painting. Tall yellow donkey ears, sloppily painted, rose from the top of Josh's head.

"I'll skin 'em alive!" Aunt Bert vowed,

her voice breaking. "Just you see if I don't! They'll be sorry sights when I get through with 'em!"

Vannie turned the light toward her aunt, expecting to see tears. But Aunt Bert wasn't crying. She looked mad enough to take off like a rocket.

"I'm goin' in and call Jeff Engel this minute," she sputtered. "Oh, that boy is goin' to regret this! Spoilin' that beautiful paintin', makin' a mockery of our Josh . . ."

Off she went, stomping across the yard and into the house with Vannie right behind her. The old lady was trembling so much that Vannie had to look up the number for her and dial it. But as soon as Mr. Engel's deep voice said hello, Aunt Bert snatched the phone and began shouting.

"Do you know what that scamp of yours has been up to?" she bellowed. "Do you know what he's done?"

And then she stopped. Mr. Engel's slow deep voice was like a growl at the other end of the line. Aunt Bert listened for what seemed like a long time, her lips in a tight line, her blue eyes shooting sparks.

"You just do that!" she exclaimed when the growl finally stopped. "Because if you don't, I will!" She listened again for a moment or two. "See you first thing in the mornin' then," she snapped, and hung up.

"Ha!" she exclaimed with satisfaction. "Jeff Engel caught that wicked boy sneakin' in just a couple of minutes ago with yellow paint all over his jeans. He has a bloody nose and a mess of bumps from head to toe, too. And he was lookin' over his shoulder to see if the sheriff was comin'! He was so scared that he couldn't confess fast enough. He and Bill Barker are the ones who drew those pictures on the windows and slashed my tires and broke my vase and my papa's rockin' chair. Seems like he thought the sheriff would figure it all out and he'd better tell his pa the whole story quick, before somebody else did."

"But why did they do those mean things?" Vannie wondered.

"Thought he was helpin' his pa," Aunt Bert said disgustedly. "Thought he could scare me so I'd go live somewhere else and let the Engels have my land. As if I would!" She slapped her hands together with such force that Vannie jumped. "As if those whippersnappers could scare me!"

But they *had* scared her, Vannie thought. The window pictures and the slashed tires and the masked face had scared her a lot.

"I s'pose I should thank you for findin' out who the villains are and scarin' 'em off," the old lady said grumpily. "But you shouldn't have gone outside, just the same. I told you to stay in the house with the door locked, and I meant it. Pure foolishness, takin' a chance like that." She scowled, but there was a look in the blue eyes that told Vannie her aunt didn't disapprove quite as much as she pretended.

For the next half hour they sat at the kitchen table drinking milk and eating raisin cookies. Aunt Bert talked about what a wicked world it was and how much better things had been when she was a girl.

"But we fixed 'em," she said. "We showed 'em you can't pick on an old lady and get away with it. Not *this* old lady anyway!"

Vannie nodded and yawned. She didn't care if Aunt Bert took most of the credit for solving the mystery of the prowlers. She was just glad they wouldn't have to be afraid anymore. She could move back to the bed on the side porch without wondering whether a masked face might suddenly peer through the screen.

Later, curled up on the daybed, she stared at the stars and tried not to think about how much nicer it would have been if Muffy were with her. He had loved sleeping on the side porch as much as she did. Then, halfway between waking and sleeping, she remembered that Aunt Bert had said she had some news. In all the excitement, she had forgotten to tell what it was, and Vannie had forgotten to ask.

Chapter 13

Aunt Bert's News

"I'm sorry," Matt Engel mumbled. "Honest."

His father poked him in the shoulder. "Speak up."

"I shouldn't have done all that stuff," Matt continued in a slightly louder voice. He was staring at a hole in the linoleum as if it were the most interesting thing he'd ever seen. Vannie almost felt sorry for him, till she remembered how he'd frightened her.

"You bet your boots you shouldn't have done it!" Aunt Bert snapped.

"What else?" Mr. Engel gave him another poke.

"My dad's goin' to pay for your tires, and Billy and I are goin' to pay him back with our allowances," Matt said.

"And what about my papa's rockin' chair?" Aunt Bert demanded. "One of the rockers is split. And the vase?"

"I'll fix the chair myself," Mr. Engel said. "We'll take it with us when we leave. And I'll get a sign painter to come out and clean up the painting on your barn." He gave Matt a disgusted look. "We'll take care of it today, and this kid can pay me for that, too—and a new vase! You pick one out and let us know the price."

"Well then." Aunt Bert nodded approval. "But we'd better not have any more trouble."

"You won't," Mr. Engel promised. "Matt, say it."

Matt looked up from the hole in the li-

noleum and took a deep breath. There
were tears in his eyes. "We Engels don't
go around scarin' people," he said, sound-
ing as if he'd practiced the line a few
times. "I really am sorry."

Even Aunt Bert seemed satisfied with
this apology. "I'll show you the rockin'
chair," she announced. "It's out on the
porch. We cleaned up the rest of the mess
ourselves, Vannie and me."

A few minutes later the chair had been
loaded into the back of the pickup, and the
truck was rolling out of the yard.

Vannie watched it go and then followed
Aunt Bert back into the house. She felt
sort of lost now that the excitement was
over.

Aunt Bert headed for the kitchen.
"That's that," she said briskly. "I guess
we taught that scallawag a lesson he'll remember."

"Guess so," Vannie agreed. She stopped
short as Aunt Bert whirled around, her
hands on her skinny hips.

"Just thought of what we have to do this afternoon," she said abruptly. "We have to go visitin', that's what."

Vannie was amazed. Except for church meetings, Aunt Bert didn't have much to do with other people. "I told you I had some news. One of the ladies at the church meeting yesterday said that her neighbor—that's deaf old Sarah Corman—has a new pet. Seems a little shrimp of a white dog came to her door one day and raised such a horrible ruckus that even she was able to hear him. He's been at her house ever since."

Vannie couldn't speak. She could hardly breathe. All she could do was stand there staring into Aunt Bert's blue eyes.

"Now don't go gettin' your hopes up too much," her aunt warned. "There may be nothin' to it. But when I heard that bit about the horrible ruckus, I did think it sounded a lot like you-know-who."

Chapter 14

Coco

Aunt Bert insisted on having lunch before they went to see Mrs. Corman.

"You can't just knock on a person's door at noon and say you've come to visit. They'll think they have to feed you lunch. At least, that's the way it is in the country. Maybe city folks don't *worry* about such things."

Vannie was so excited, she didn't care if she was being insulted. *A little shrimp of a white dog who raised a horrible ruckus . . .* Who else could it be but Muffy? He was safe! They would be together again this very afternoon. She was sure of it.

Aunt Bert ate two slices of bread and cheese for lunch and drank two cups of coffee. She was a very slow eater. Vannie forced down half of a peanut-butter sandwich and spilled her glass of milk.

"I shouldn't have told you where we were goin'," Aunt Bert grumbled as they mopped up the milk. "Never thought you'd get in such a state! Well, you'll just have to wait a little longer. I'm not goin' callin' in blue jeans, and that's that."

When they were finally in the car and rattling down the highway, Vannie couldn't sit still. "Where does Mrs. Corman live?" she wanted to know. "Is it very far from here?"

"Sit back," Aunt Bert ordered. "We won't get there any faster if you fall out the door. Sarah lives this side of town. A couple of miles along this road and then down a little side lane. Her mama and mine were friends a long time ago."

A couple of miles. That wouldn't be too far for Muffy to have traveled. As Aunt Bert slowed the car and turned onto a gravel road, Vannie began to wish the drive had taken longer. As long as she didn't know for sure, she could go on hoping.

"That's Sarah Corman's place." Aunt Bert pointed at a little white house at the edge of the road. It looked freshly painted, and there were tubs of red geraniums on either side of the front steps.

"Might as well get out," Aunt Bert went on when Vannie didn't move. "This is what we came for—and besides, somebody already knows we're here. Listen."

Vannie listened. From inside the little house came a high-pitched barking that grew even louder and more frantic as she leaped out of the car and raced up the porch steps. The lace curtains were pushed aside and a little white poodle looked out. When he saw Vannie on the porch, he threw himself against the glass and barked more loudly than ever.

"Horrible ruckus is right," grumbled Aunt Bert, but Vannie paid no attention. She didn't even say hello to the white-haired old lady who opened the door. All her attention was on the dog that scooted between the old lady's legs and leaped into Vannie's arms.

"MUFFY!"

Vannie sat down with a thump right on the doorstep and hugged her dog. Muffy licked her face, her arms, and her fingers, squealing with delight.

"My stars and garters!" Aunt Bert exclaimed. "What a way to behave!" She stepped around Vannie, into the little entrance hall. "Sarah, this is my grand-niece Vannie Kirkland. Sorry about her manners. She knows better, I *think*. Vannie, stand up here and say hello to Mrs. Corman."

Vannie scrambled to her feet with Muffy in her arms. "Pleased to meet you," she murmured, petting Muffy's silky head.

"Louder," Aunt Bert whispered. "And look up so she can read your lips."

"Pleased to meet you," Vannie repeated.

"I'm pleased to meet you, too," Mrs. Corman said warmly. "No need to tell me why you're here. I just knew the folks who owned Coco would claim him sooner or later. He must have wandered away, I told myself. Nobody'd let a scrap of a dog like that run around loose on purpose. So I just decided to keep him safe until you came."

She led them into a cozy living room and told them to sit down. "I was just pouring out some ice-cold apple juice when I heard Coco barking," she said. "I'll bring it right in."

Vannie sat at one end of the couch with Muffy on her lap. Aunt Bert sat in a straight-backed chair, her feet barely touching the carpet. Mrs. Corman went out to the kitchen but kept right on talking.

"I just want you to know how much I've enjoyed having Coco here with me," she said. "He's the smartest little dog ever!"

Aunt Bert rolled her eyes.

"Every time someone's at the door, he tells me, just like he did with you folks today. Lots of times I don't hear the newsboy or the mailman when I'm here by myself, but Coco hears them. Just yesterday I was out in the yard when my daughter telephoned. I didn't hear the phone, but that little dog came to the door and barked and barked till I came back inside. I can't talk on the phone, of course—can't hear a word—but my daughter calls every day, and if I don't pick up the phone and say hello she gets upset and drives seven miles to make sure I'm all right. Muffy's saved her a lot of trips. And that's not all!"

Aunt Bert leaned back with a sigh, as if she'd heard more than enough, but Vannie listened eagerly. After a moment or two Muffy wiggled out of her grasp and dived into a basket at the other end of the sofa.

"Just last night," Mrs. Corman continued, "I thought I'd make myself a piece of toast before bedtime, and do you know, the pop-up thing on the toaster stuck. I never noticed it, but all of a sudden there was Coco barking like crazy at the smoke pouring out of the toaster. If he hadn't warned me, I don't know what would have happened. I really do think he kept the house from burning down."

At that, Aunt Bert groaned out loud. Vannie slid the length of the couch to pat Muffy's head.

"There now, Coco is showing you his bed," Mrs. Corman said proudly, coming in from the kitchen with a tray of glasses. "I put a pillow in that basket the first evening he was here, and he jumped right in like he knew it was for him." She smiled at Vannie. "I could tell he came from a good home, being so well behaved and all. I knew someone must be missing him a lot."

"I was," Vannie said softly. "I sure was."

"It was nice of you to take him in, Sarah," Aunt Bert said politely. "He could have got in big trouble runnin' around the countryside by himself."

Silence fell as they sipped their apple juice. Then Muffy leaped out of his basket in a flurry of yips and flew to the footstool in front of the front window.

"Must be the mailman," Mrs. Corman said. "You see how he notices everything?"

Vannie set her glass carefully on the little woven mat Mrs. Corman had put on the end table. She felt tears brimming up in her eyes, and she didn't know why. She just knew she had to be by herself for a while.

"I'll get your mail if you want me to," she offered.

Mrs. Corman looked pleased. "Thank you so much, Annie dear," she said. "It's the box right across the road."

Vannie hurried out, not bothering to explain that she was Vannie, not Annie. And Muffy was Muffy, not Coco. What difference did names make? She crossed the gravel road and took her time taking the mail from the box, one piece at a time. A catalog. A bill from the electric company.

A letter. She thought of the letter her mom had sent from California—the letter that hadn't mentioned Muffy at all. For the first time she admitted to herself that Aunt Bert was right. There wasn't going to be a place for Muffy in California—not for a while, anyway. Vannie's mom hadn't mentioned him in her letter because *she didn't know what to say.*

Slowly, Vannie walked back across the road and up the little walk between the pots of geraniums. She could hear Muffy barking excitedly and bouncing against the front door. By the time she had opened the door and the little dog had jumped into her arms again, she had made up her mind.

"Here's your mail," she said softly. "And here's Coco. He can stay with you if you want him."

Aunt Bert gasped. Mrs. Corman took the letters and the dog and then glanced at Vannie sharply. "What was that you said, dear?"

Vannie cleared her throat and said it again, in a loud but shaky voice. "Coco can stay with you, if you'd like to have him. It's okay."

Mrs. Corman looked at her unbelievingly. "I don't understand," she protested. "He's your dog, Annie. It's very sweet of you, dear, but I know you love him."

Vannie shook her head. Now that she'd said Muffy could stay, she felt empty inside and unable to say more.

"The child's goin' to move to California with her folks soon," Aunt Bert explained. "There might not be room for the dog at their new place." She spoke loudly and slowly so Mrs. Corman would understand, but she was looking at Vannie, almost as if she'd never seen her before.

"Oh! Oh my!" Mrs. Corman put Coco in his basket and gave Vannie a big hug. She looked as if she'd like to hug Aunt Bert, too, but didn't quite dare.

"We'd better get on home now," Aunt Bert said quickly. "I've got a wash to do."

Mrs. Corman carried Muffy out to the kitchen and closed the door. Vannie could hear him barking and leaping against the kitchen door as they walked out to the car.

"I'm sure Coco will never forget his Annie," Mrs. Corman said, reaching in through the car window to hug Vannie one more time. "And neither will I, dear. Thank you very much."

She stepped back, and Aunt Bert started the motor. Slowly, they bounced down the road away from the little white house.

"Well, well," Aunt Bert said when they reached the highway. "Ain't you the one for surprises!"

Vannie didn't say anything. She couldn't. She was glad she had given Muffy to Mrs. Corman, and she knew they would be happy together. But she ached. It was like a stomachache and a headache and a toothache all mixed up together, but worse than any of them. She felt as if she might die of it.

Chapter 15

A Midnight Surprise

"You asleep?"

"No."

"Didn't think you would be." Aunt Bert stood at the kitchen door peering out at the daybed, where Vannie lay scrunched up in a ball. "Come on, get up. I can't sleep neither."

Vannie rolled out of bed and padded, barefoot, into the kitchen. She was glad to leave her damp pillow and tangled-up sheets.

An open notebook covered with numbers lay on the kitchen table. "I've been thinkin' some deep thoughts," Aunt Bert said. She poured two glasses of milk and put some raisin cookies on a plate. "And I've been figurin'."

Vannie sighed. She'd been thinking some pretty deep thoughts herself.

"Mostly," Aunt Bert continued, "I've been thinkin' about you. How you stayed here without a fuss when your folks wanted you to. How you gave Sarah Corman the dog. You're tough, same as me, but you know which way the wind is blowin', and you make the best of it. That's something I never did learn."

Vannie wondered if Aunt Bert was paying her a compliment. Probably not.

"Anyway." Her aunt moved the sheet of numbers in front of her and glared at it. "I've been thinkin' I just might sell a parcel of land to Jeff Engel—only a parcel, mind you—and have me some cash, for once. I could buy a brand-new secondhand

car, before the old one falls apart on the highway. And I could get a dog to keep me company after you go off to California. I was thinkin' of a golden retriever puppy. Like Josh." She scowled at the paper. "If I got him right away, you could give me a hand trainin' him the rest of the summer. If you want to, that is."

Vannie leaned back in her chair. The tightness around her heart loosened just a little, and she took a deep breath.

"I guess I could help you," she said, trying to sound offhand. "I trained Muffy."

"That's not sayin' much," Aunt Bert snorted, but she looked up from the paper with a sort of smile as she said it.

Vannie smiled back, sort of, and the tight feeling loosened some more. A puppy! He would lick her cheek to wake her up in the morning, and at night he'd sleep curled up in a warm ball against her stomach. He wouldn't *know* anything. She'd have to teach him not to touch Aunt

A Midnight Surprise

Bert's treasures and show him how to keep out of the way of Elvis. He'd have to learn about raccoons and bumblebees, too.

She wondered if the summer would be long enough to get it all done.